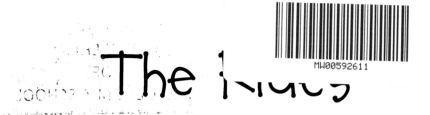

The Rides

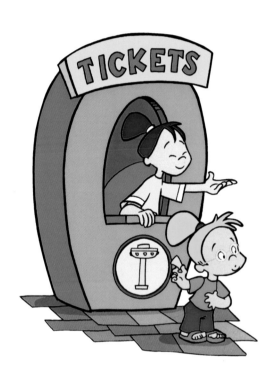

Illustrated by Rodney Selby

Rigby

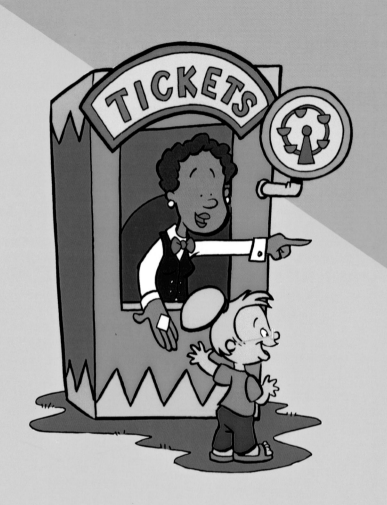

You can get on
the red seat.

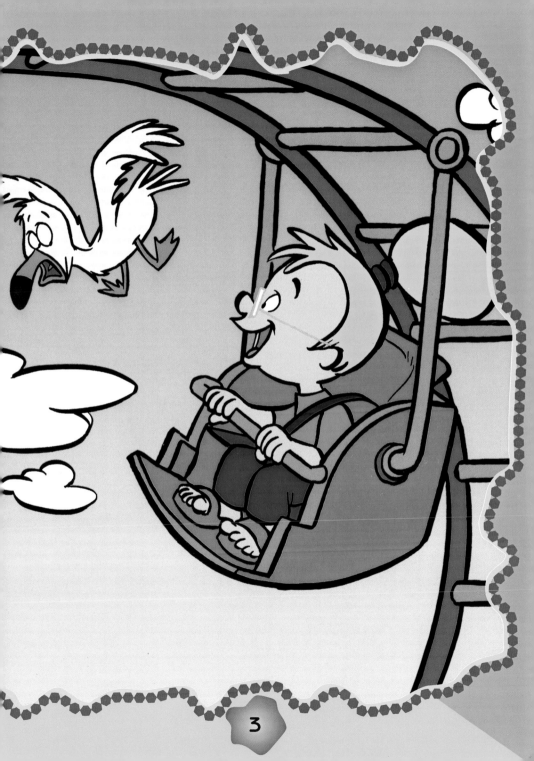

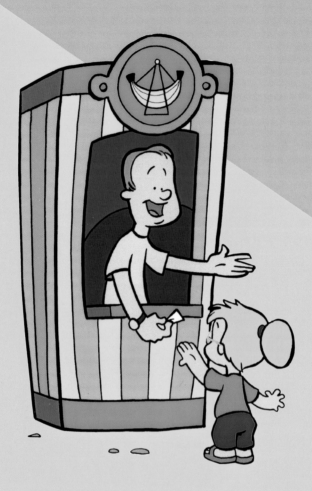

You can get on
the green seat.

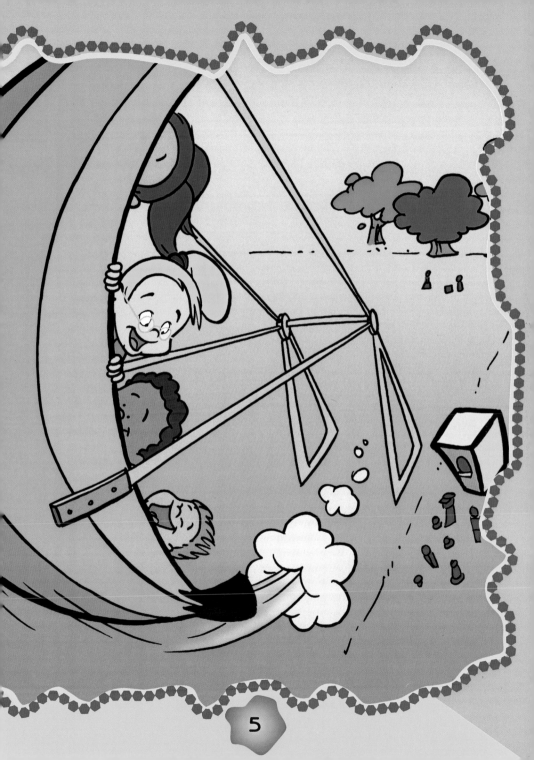

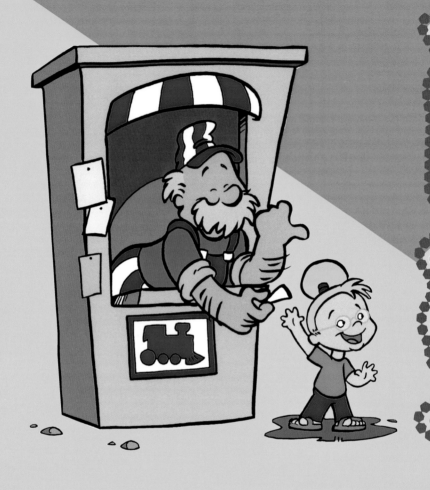

You can get on
the blue seat.

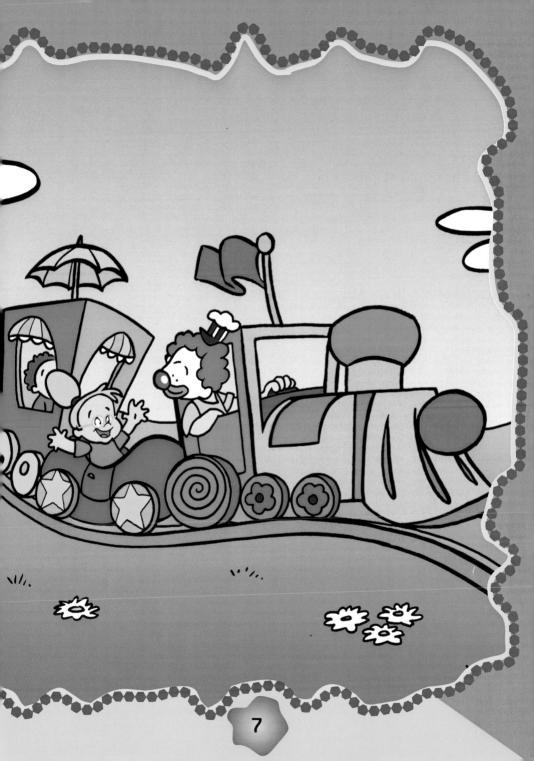

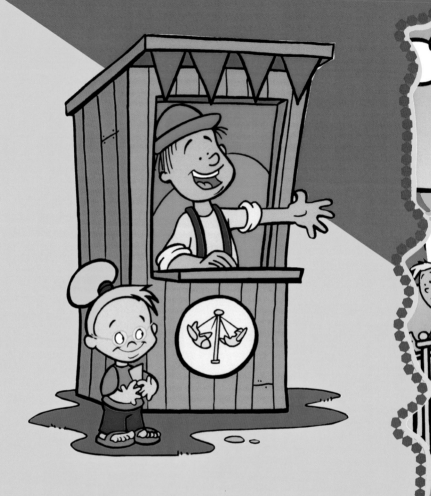

You can get on
the black seat.

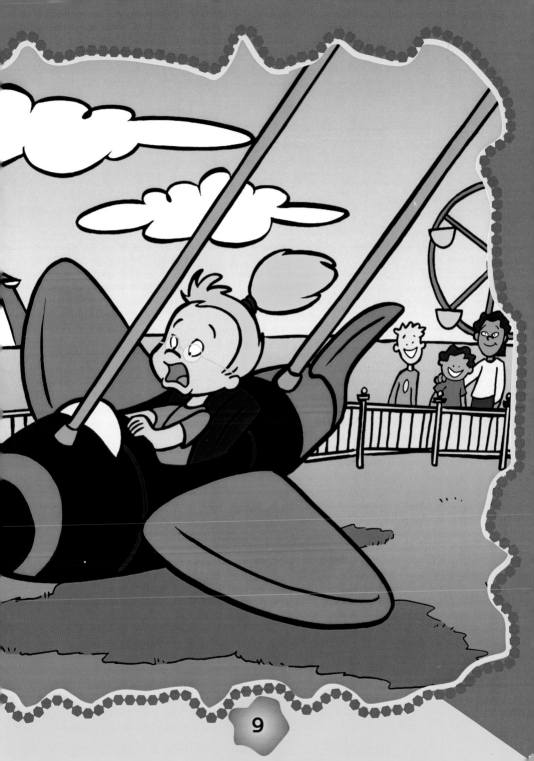

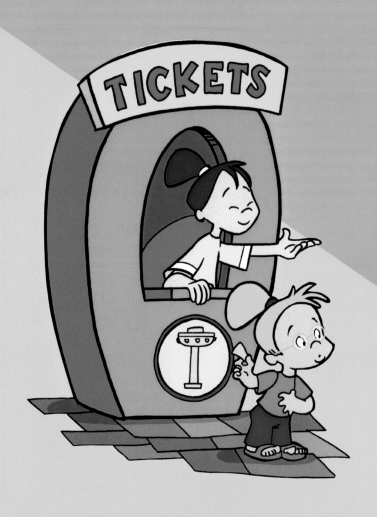

You can get on
the orange seat.

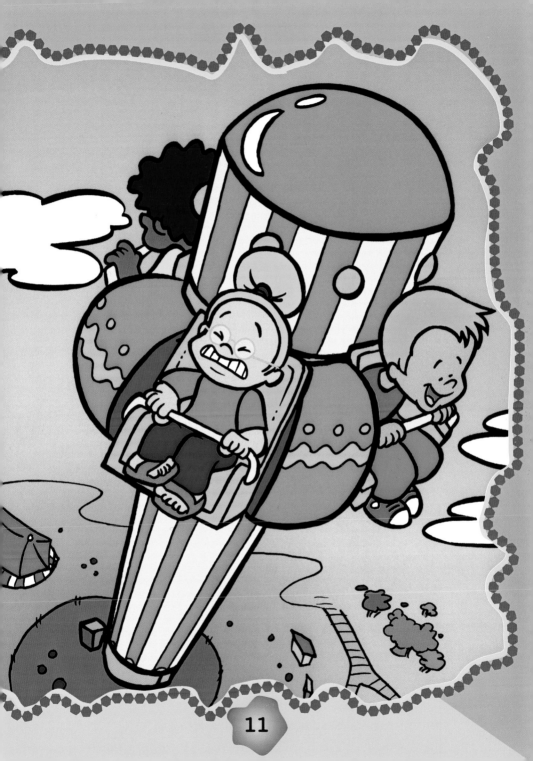

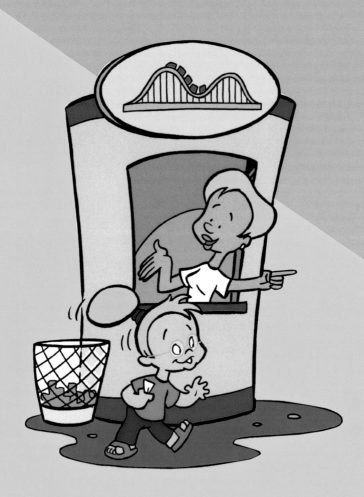

You can get on
the purple seat.

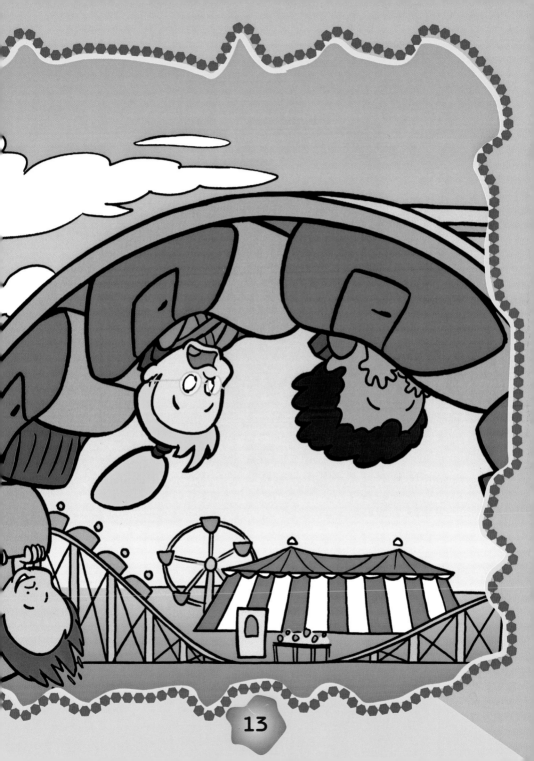

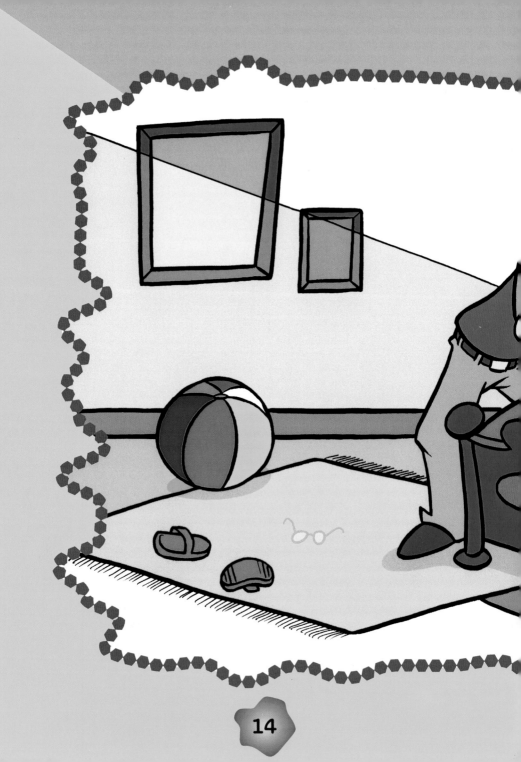

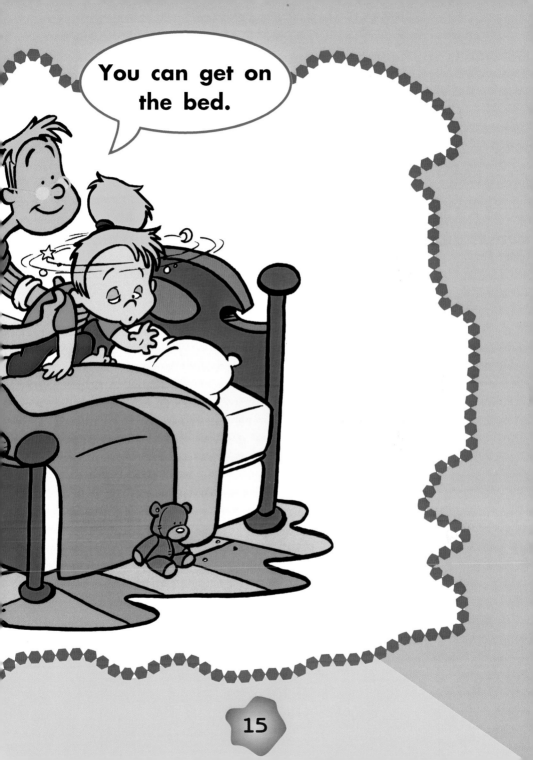

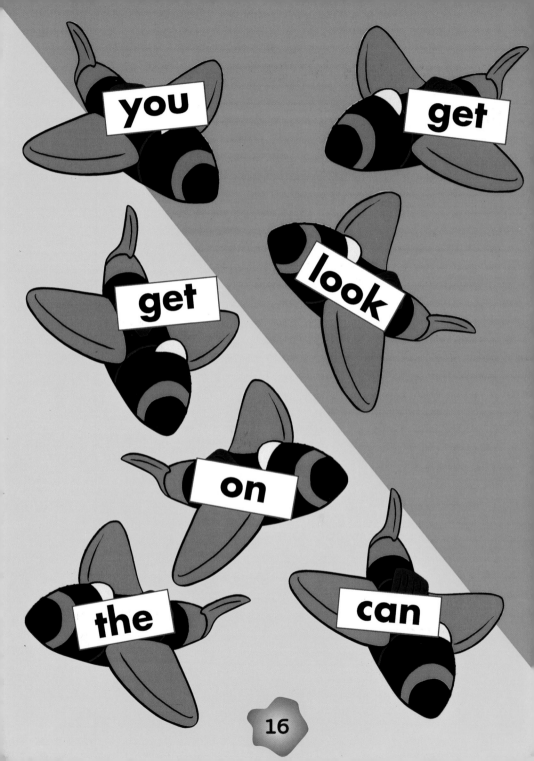